Where's Sancho?
III

Don Quiett

My Name is Irrelevant: A Two Act Play

Inquires concerning all rights should be sent to P.O. Box 271,
Fuquay–Varina, North Carolina 27526

Published by Modern Aesthete

Cover artwork by William Albert Corbett
Cover design by Cari Corbett

Printed in the United States of America

First Edition

ISBN: 978-0-6151-6678-0

Dedicated to Grandpa Albert (Pampamp) Kennedy
and
Uncle Al (William Albert) Corbett

Acknowledgements

I thank modern writers whose insights continually affect my writing. These are: David Sirota, Joe Conason, Norman Solomon, Mark Miller and Robert Kennedy, Jr.

MY NAME IS IRRELEVANT

by

Don Quiett

(Two Act Play)

SETTING:
Present day hobos, people of the road, outcasts are gathered under a city road overpass. They consist of an outsourced or redundant computer engineer, a textile worker, a steel worker, a teacher, an environmentalist and assorted beings who never really made it into civilization's 'defined' circle of acceptance. Their clothing is old, tattered by time. They're relics of their past. This group is neither ignorant nor illiterate, just non–game players of life. They are amorphous, representing all ethnicities, races, genders and yet none. True invisible people of the streets. Dinner is waited for, dog being slowly roasted on spit over a fire. For warmth, old tin barrels are employed as furnaces.

The overpass occupies about 2/3 of the stage. Above the overpass is a screen for projections or slides. Initially, a big city is seen (slide 1001). The rest of the stage has a smaller screen showing a tree bound park (like Central Park, NY or a local area park). As the play proceeds, various photos will appear on the larger and smaller screens, alternating, as indicated, and then go back to the original big city park photos. Slides, in essence, overlay acting, so both occur simultaneously. The play was designed to function with all the projections recommended or some or none of them. However, the closing projections are a must and are necessary to the play.

CHARACTERS:
Jacque – textile worker (speaks with French accent)
Petie – computer programmer, analyst (speaks with deep, preacher, lecturing voice)
Maggie – college teacher, environmentalist (reader's voice)
Iain – general handyman (speaks with high pitch and rapid, nervous voice)
Matt – ex-soldier (sounds like Eeyore from Winnie the Pooh – talks slowly)
Susej – (called Irrelevant in Act II), no one knows much about him; pronounced Sue Say (whispers or soft voice)
Lew – blind, old tailor (speaks with rough, gravelly voice)
Nick – ex-steel worker ((has southern accent)

S.P. – 'Retired' CEO (speaks with loud, but a happy, uplifting voice)
Detective I.B. Leeown – dedicated police detective (Bogart-like or Edward G. Robinson-like voice – tough sounding)

ACT I

As the curtain rises, the photo above the overpass, on the big screen, is a picture of the overpass with the major city behind it. On the little screen is a picture of a park (similar to Central Park). Under the overpass, the characters are walking around, standing up, sitting down, walking over to the food spit or standing around trying to keep warm by the fire.

CURTAIN RISES

SUSEJ (said Sue Say)
(*Sitting, leaning back on the inclined wall looking up at the overpass away from the fire, talking loudly to no one in particular*) Christians? Christians, Christians? Should be ashamed?!! (*Said with rising voice so seems as a question*)

JACQUE
Shit. Let it go. Always with the religious crap. Give it a break. Christians are Christians.

SUSEJ
That's no answer.

PETIE
Geesh! Jacque's right. Besides, what the hell kind of name is Susej anyway? Should at least know that if to share dog together, commune. (*Turns the makeshift spit*)

IAIN

(*Jumps up and nervously walks around*) God hater! You just hate God. Why? Don't believe?

SUSEJ

(*Calmly*) Well, as to the name, my dad fought in all of those Mideast wars. Saw the name somewhere, liked it, called Mom, voila. And who mentioned God, Iain? I didn't.

IAIN

Yes you did! You said Christians.

SUSEJ

That's not God.

Laughter all around.

IAIN

(*Angry, hesitant*) Blasphemers. They do – lots of – good stuff. Like feed us sometimes.

SUSEJ

Do–gooders! Is that what the red print means? To be a do–gooder?

IAIN, PETIE, MAGGIE, JACQUE

Huh? Red?

SUSEJ

God!? Haven't you read it? The Bible and junk?

PETIE

Hold on now, junk? (*Looks angry, stares down at Susej*) You mean that English king's creation? Where scholars, priests gathered to agree on some new translation? By a two thirds vote?

MAGGIE
How do you know this stuff?

IAIN
What do you mean – got together?

PETIE
(*Gesturing wildly*) Well, I wasn't always boing, man of the streets, homeless. Computer technology was my bag. Was outsourced. Dumped, expendable, trashed. But I do remember Jesus's words were printed in red. (*Ponders, looks to heaven, clasps his hands skyward*) I wish I had a copy now.

Thunder, a banging noise, fog. Stage left a loud metallic voice says "Here" and a book flies through the air to his feet. All look in amazement. Petie slowly walks over and reverently picks up the book. It opens up to a page.

ALL
What the H– – –. Man, did you – – –. Amazing – – –. Maybe I should become a Chr – – –.

JACQUE
Read it. It's a sign.

EVERYONE
(*Silently stare at the book*) Come on.

PETIE
Piss off, Jacque. This is weird.

JACQUE
Read!

PETIE
Back off! Let me think. My first thought is – I don't know.

JACQUE

What's it say? Come on! It's a sign.

PETIE

(*Picks up and reads. Mumbles to self while pacing, stops*)
Christ! It's all about love! The red stuff!

MAGGIE

Piss off is right. Who would – does – love our sorry asses?
(*Mumbling*) Life's burdens.

SUSEJ

You sound like a Republican.

Maggie grunts.

PETIE

No listen, it's in red. (*Reads to himself, mumbling at first*)
Love your enemies, bless them that curse you, do good——

IAIN

Shutup with that dribble.

JACQUE

Them's nice words.

IAIN

Yeah. For who? The rich? Secure?

MAGGIE

Does sound like Republican propaganda. Ha! Bombed the
shit out of those A–rabs, though. (*Laughing*) Lots of love
there and look what did to us!

IAIN

(*Laughing*) God damn right. Deserved it.

SUSEJ
(*Contemplatively*) Makes you wonder though, doesn't it?

A long pause.

JACQUE
(*Exasperated*) What!

SUSEJ
Oh, just wondering whether Christians, anyone, ever read the Book's red. Cripes.

PETIE
(*Flipping through pages of the book*) This is weird. Zap! Book! Well, here's another one, in red I might add. "It's easier for a camel to go through the eye of a needle than for a rich man to get into the kingdom of God." Damn, mentioned multiple times.

MAGGIE
(*Laughing*) Tell that to the Republicans. Hell, to all politicians, corporate boardrooms. Missed that one – for sure.

IAIN
Yeah, take the pay gap. What, 400 times now? When born, hear there was only 20 times difference between the CEO's and worker's pay. I can see the sign now on the pearly gates. (*Holds hands up as if reading*) CEOs need not apply!

JACQUE
I read a book once –

MAGGIE
One is better than none.

JACQUE

Buggar off! Anyway, in English History– by the way, weird people, the English– anyway, around the 1200s, said if you read the Bible, translated into English that is, you were burned at the stake. The crime – a blas–phem–er.

IAIN

Bullshit. Translated from what?

JACQUE

No. No. (*Laughing*) After the peasants read it, realized they didn't need the priests, could pray direct to the MAN. Circumvent them. Bad for priest business.

MAGGIE

Republicans, I bet. Corner the God market. Their God or the burning pit.

IAIN

This is boring. Can we talk about something else?

JACQUE

Wait a minute.

IAIN

For what? Besides, we need more firewood if this fire's to last the night. I'll get it. (*Gets up, breaks chair or old wooden box. Show slides while does*)

Screen 1002 – Alternate slides starting with Big Screen. Begin as Iain says, "This is boring – – –."

Big Screen	Little Screen
Flat world	*Thing > 6000 yrs old (as Dinosaur)*
Galileo	*Chastity belt*
Bosch–Heaven/Hell Painting	*Old science example*

Sun going around Earth

(Internet provides a source of photo that could be used, with appropriate authorization.)

JACQUE

Does that there Good Book say anything about the great moral issue that divides the country today – abortion, or better put, when life starts?

SUSEJ

Damn. Talk about déjà vu. I remember this topic in Sunday School.

JACQUE

You studied abortion in Sunday School?

SUSEJ

(*Laughing*) No, no, life's beginning. Said something about it. Genesis 2:7 or 7:2. Why I recall, I don't know.

MAGGIE

Thought you were kicked out. A church flunky.

SUSEJ

Yeah, said I questioned too much. Doubting Thomas was not, as I was told, a good role model. At 9, condemned to the fires of Hell. Strict Presbyterian preachers. (Shakes head)

MAGGIE

You're kidding, right?

SUSEJ

No. Like that pig story. The one where evil demons, or whatever, were zapped into pigs who then plunged over a cliff. My question – what'd the farmer do? Bankrupted him. Why I was told, Satan was within me, to ask such a thing. Doomed.

MAGGIE
Guess no point to being good after that. No hope. God's clinched fist – burning pit – awesome for a kid's little mind.

SUSEJ
(*Opens his hand*) Only a matter of time. Hell awaited me.

PETIE
Damn. You're scary sometimes, Susej. 2:7 says, "And the Lord God formed man of the dust of the ground and breathed into his nostrils the breath of life; and man became a living soul."

MAGGIE
Wow! Sounds like – take a breath and get a soul. Clearly the beginning to me.

IAIN
This is stupid. Too simple. Simple minded.

PETIE
(*Reading quickly, flipping pages*) The red stuff refers to poor, sick, old, meek, and how all should care for all. No high or low. Rich or poor. All equal.

MAGGIE
Is He advocating socialism? Communism?

IAIN
Doubt it.

Maggie

People–ism, emanating from an expanded Bill of Rights is
what we need. A new – 'ism'. And not cabalism, oh, I
mean capitalism.

SUSEJ

Let's go with Iain and subject change. Petie, any chance
IBM will in–source instead of outsource?

PETIE

(*Laughing with sneer and looks to heaven*) Pwuuuu.
(*Blows air out of his mouth, picks up crumpled paper*)
Reading from my crinkled up blanket, of last night, they're
laying another 1500 off. But the good news, the paper said,
IBM's profit and stocks were up.

MAGGIE

(*Stands, raises hands and give speech like politician*) My
fellow Americans, government should be run like a
business. I'm a product of that policy, so my experience will
be invaluable if elected. You too can – – – (*Stops, slumps*)
Yeah, you too. Government and business. Not a good mix,
I think. Do you know the top 300,000 people in the
United States make as much as the bottom 150 <u>million</u>,
combined! Need that camel story tattooed on their
foreheads– so can read it daily.

*Screen 1003 – Start showing while Maggie speaks, end during
Susej. Alternate screens.*

Big Screen	*Little Screen*
Bread lines	*Textile industry*
Closed banks	*Steel industry*
Wall Street	*Train industry*
Railway Barons	*Homeless on streets*

SUSEJ

Got my vote Maggie, if I can find a place to vote! Jacque, penny, well considering inflation, dollar for your thoughts? You look spaced.

JACQUE

Sorry. Thinking about my wife. Our troubles started even before all of this economic chaos.

IAIN

Can say that again. Chaos. National debt, trade debt, pension plan debt, budget debt – debt – debt – debt.

PETIE

Stop it.

IAIN

Piss off.

PETIE

(*Hears sirens in the distance*) Man, hear that? Sounds like the whole force is out tonight. Sirens everywhere.

SUSEJ

Yeah, but not close. No problem.

MAGGIE

Wonder what's up? Does sound like more than usual.

SUSEJ

Go on, Jacque, the floor is yours.

JACQUE

(*Anger builds as he speaks*) Fish. I hate fish, damn fish.

IAIN

What? (*Laughs*) What the fu – – –

MAGGIE
(*Interrupting*) Not what I expected. Good start, though.
Definitely not a boring start.

JACQUE
Yeah, hate the little bastards. Love to fish, though.

IAIN
Thought you were going to tell us about some runaway
wife. A real fish story. Not a REAL fish story.

JACQUE
Told you it was boring.

*Turns away and stops talking, new character stumbles into scene
bumping into Petie.*

PETIE
What the hell?

MATT
Oucha ell eee. (*Weak, wimpy, mumbly voice. What he's
trying to say is "would you help me" but he mumbles*)

PETIE
Who the hell are you? We don't tolerate drunks here, so
move on! Or I'll bash your brains in. Go on– get. (*Pushes
him away and falls*)

SUSEJ
Stop, Petie. Stop! (*Jumps up and stops Matt's fall
somewhat*)

PETIE
You know the rule.

SUSEJ

It's not that.

MATT

Gym ooul ox ounuts ooohyuder. (*Saying "gave me whole box of doughnuts, do–gooder."*)

SUSEJ

OK, OK.

MAGGIE

You understood that?

SUSEJ

Ya, some do–gooder gave him a box of doughnuts.

MAGGIE

(*Excited*) All right!

SUSEJ

No, Matt's a diabetic. He probably ate the whole damn box. Hard not to when starving. Diabetic or not.

They lay him down, cover him up with some old newspapers.

MAGGIE

God, his breath does smell like he's been on a binge. Really stinks.

SUSEJ

That's his only hope. Piss toxins out, breathe 'em out. Budget cuts killed his treatment. If he starts shaking, we'll go to emergency. No use until then.

Screen 1004 – As take care of Matt and before Susej requests fish story again, show following.

Big Screen	*Little Screen*
Poor hungry lines	*Hoover hard times*
(2 or 3)	
Food lines	*Child labor*
Nursing home	*Street people*
Tenement housing	*Out of gas, signs of*
	depression

Matt is put in secure bedding where all can observe him, and are quiet for a while, busying themselves with camp stuff.

SUSEJ

(*Blurts out after a while of silence*) Fish. I'm on pins and needles. (*Starts chanting and all join in*)
Fish. We want fish. Fish. We want fish.

Sirens blare up. All pause and look.

SUSEJ

Relax people. Go on, Jacque. We apparently have the time.

JACQUE

Well as I said, fish – – –.

IAIN

Fish again. Where's the wife?

JACQUE

Dead!

All fall silent. Iain squirms, looks sheepish and apologizes with gestures and not words.

JACQUE

She ate all my fish, she loved fish; breaded fish, fried, any preparation worked for her, even sushi style.

IAIN

Yuck. She ate bait?

MAGGIE

Please! Grow up.

JACQUE

Then, don't really know when, but it started. Tired all the time. Weak. She slept a lot. So to make her feel better, I fished more, so she had more pleasing fish to eat. Damn, I hate fish.   (*Pauses a good while*)

IAIN

Fish's good for you, right? Protein. Healthy.

JACQUE

Oh, yeah. It helped. I killed her!

MAGGIE

What? You murdered your wife?

IAIN

Get away, Maggie. Jacque doesn't even kill bugs. Ants and things.

JACQUE

Fish. I hate them! Hate, hate. Hate them.

IAIN

Fish again?

SUSEJ

And now the rest of the story – to quote Monty Python or somebody.

JACQUE

Toxic. Mercury! Among other stuff. Should have been a posted sign, but the powers that be didn't want business hurt. Tourism. Four little words could have saved my wife. Do not eat fish. (*Underscores words with a hand gesture*)

IAIN

Damn. (*Pauses*) Damn, damn, damn. (*Said fast*)

MAGGIE

Funny. Well, not really, more tragic. I read, somewhere, California, to not hurt business, was trying to figure out and legislate, what the permissible level of lead in candy should be. Believe it!?

SUSEJ

(*Shocked*) It's accumulative! 0 is the answer. Remember lead paint? Should we bring it back?

Screen 1005 – Start with Susej and end with Maggie's question about Republican kids. Alternate screen.

Big Screen	Little Screen
Polluted air	Garbage dump
Polluted water	Burning river (Hudson, Cleveland)
Dead fish in river	Traffic jam on interstate
Computer dump	Toxic dump
– millions in a pile	

MAGGIE

Well, it seems popular candy fireballs owe their burning sensation to a special pepper grown in Mexico. On polluted land! Recalling the candies – out. And, aaaand stopping production – out. Legislation – in.

PETIE

Ha! So, legislation saying candy's OK, if less than point 0T– 0T – 0T–1 milligrams – dawns. See it now. Yep.

MAGGIE

And not just 4 little words. Do not eat pepper candy. All that's needed.

IAIN

Wait, isn't that's 5!

MAGGIE

Piss off. Pleeesssee. (*Stretches out arms*) My question– <u>Are there no Republican kids</u>! Laws they make, they <u>can't</u> have kids. That's public/business unions, ventures, for ya.

JACQUE

Tough titties. Anyway, we spent all our money and more trying to save my wife.

MAGGIE

But I thought textile workers got good benefits. Union and all.

JACQUE

Boop! Wrong. Before the company left the country, benefits went first. Cost savings, they said. Lie! Either way, I went broke, wife died and whammo, I'm here. My dad would say God's punishing me?

SUSEJ

God doesn't work that way. I recall a classmate got lice, and his dad beat the shit out of him. Why? God was punishing him with lice, so it's proof he did wrong. Some dad. Kid did nothing wrong.

MAGGIE

Bastards.

IAIN

Quick wit. Well Maggie, what's your story? Face it, the night's young.

MAGGIE

Doubt if you really care. (*Pause*) Hell, whatever, I'm a tree hugger. Was one before it became synonymous with devil worshiping. My trouble started – – –. (*Thinks hard*) Yep, with the Contract <u>on</u> America.

IAIN

Oooh, ooowh. Save the spotted owl or your job. That sucks.

MAGGIE

Put that way, yes. Besides, the owl is safe, but that's how they put it. Purple cow crap.

IAIN

What? Purple cow, shit. Aren't any.

MAGGIE

Bingo!

IAIN

Don't get it. Purple – – –

SUSEJ

Think on it, Iain. Continue Maggie, how'd you get into that?

MAGGIE

I was a fresh minted college teacher. Idealist.

IAIN

That's always bad – idealism's not real.

MAGGIE

Take a leak. (*Shakes head, mumbles to self*) Well, I
learned the hard way. Not only is government and business
a bad mix, but public and private sector ventures, as they
say in the university setting, are bad too.

IAIN

Any fish in this story?

JACQUE

Stuff it!

*Policeman runs by the group, all stop and watch. Cop goes on with
nothing said.*

IAIN

Guess we're not tonight's bait.

PETIE

Never know.

JACQUE

Too close to home.

MAGGIE

Oh well, if I may go on? Oil and mining pollution were my
interests. Bad timing, considering the White House's
interests.

IAIN

(*Agitated*) Lay off Republicans. Just because their ideas are
different than yours doesn't mean they're bad ideas, just
different.

MAGGIE

(*Holding her head and pacing*) Sucked you in. Well, after the White House put enemies of the environment in bureaucratic leadership roles, the same CEOs started buying universities.

PETIE

Can you do that?

IAIN

No. She's joking. Idealist jokes. (*Laughs*) Can't buy them things.

MAGGIE

You decide. Buying government wasn't enough. They donated to universities. Of course, with strings. They wanted their kind of research.

IAIN

What strings? Colleges are independent!

MAGGIE

No more. Public/business ventures were the key in my demise. Maybe the whole country's.

IAIN

Where's the fish? Where's the fish?

MAGGIE

Anyway, money bought academic influence. And dictatorial powers. Its dictates demanded appropriate research OR the money goes. Stop malcontented professors OR the money goes. Help business interests OR the money goes. Basic research, truth seeking research – gone. Universities needed the money. Became dependent.

IAIN

You exaggerate. This isn't Iran. Left liberal, commie, pinkos, college stuff flourishes in our country.

MAGGIE

Ya, right. I'm here under a bridge prepared to eat dog shit simply because I exaggerate. And I'm called an idealist? (*Flops on the ground*)

IAIN

Get real. Pollution is bad for business. Be honest, what did you do wrong?

MAGGIE

Had lice.

IAIN

Noooo way.

MAGGIE

Killed my tenure. Big money really big, 100s of millions, bought chairmanships, centers, and institutes.

JACQUE

So. Study what's good for business, the country.

MAGGIE

Mercury toxicity did not float. Not appropriate. Cheaper for business to just dump instead of clean up. I was a financial albatross for the university. The messenger is dead.

IAIN

(*Laughing*) Ha, ha, ha, like the canaries?

MAGGIE

Real funny, Iain. Defeated, I quit.

SUSEJ
(*Pleading*) Can't quit, Maggie. Earth needs canaries.

PETIE
(*All this time, has been reading the book and looks up speaks and interrupts*) Been reading this red stuff. It's mostly about love. Like humans should be one big family, buds. Buddies.

JACQUE
Well someone sure screwed up. Or maybe no one really did read that damn book.

PETIE
Yeah, nothing about fish on Friday, celibacy, dancing, laughing. Just love. One another.

IAIN
Just like Merlin!

All stop, are still, and stare at Iain.

What? What? (*Looks around*) You know, Excalibur, the stone, King Arthur pulls it out. Remember? Well, he only succeeded because he loved his dead father, loved the people and loved the country and would do right by all. At least that's according to Merlin.

SUSEJ
Well done, Iain. Well done. Merlin was a tree–hugger too, did you know?

Tap, tap, tapping is heard and moving closer. A blind, bearded, tattered overcoat wearing-man enters.

LEW
(*Calls out*) Is that chicken I smell cooking?

IAIN

(*Yells back*) In your dreams.

MAGGIE

Hey Lew, what's happening?

LEW

Dumb question for a blind man. Thank Christ I can't see this misery. Where's Susej? Frog?

IAIN

No, dog!

LEW

Oh. Well, can't tell a difference anyway between dog and frog. Both taste like chicken.

SUSEJ

Come join us!

LEW

Thanks.

All sit around the fire, eat. After meal, conversation picks up again.

Screen 1006 – Start showing as Lew speaks, as he questions if eating frog or dog etc. Alternate screens.

Big Screen	*Little Screen*
Merlin conjuring Excalibur	*Merlin creating fog or fire*
Tree huggers	*Amazon from distance*
Canary in cage	

LEW

That was good chicken. (*Rubs his belly and acts like had a big meal*)

IAIN

Dog!

LEW

Not for a blind man. Anyway, let me tell you something of interest; went to the district office to see our Congressman. (*Shakes head, rubs belly*) Damn, that was the best frog I had in a long time. Needed a side order of sautéed escargot or worms, though.

MAGGIE

The point, Lew? The point! Our stomachs are queasy enough.

LEW

Well, they said I couldn't come in. More precisely, said – get out!

MAGGIE

What did you expect? From a Congressman, anyway.

LEW

Saw, well heard, on the TV in the appliance shop window, him saying he's back home to talk to his – to his – con –, constit–u–ents. That's me. So I went to see him. Chit–chat.

JACQUE

God. Talk about naïveté.

Hear Petie mumbling to self.

                              LEW
Wait, what's Petie doing?

                             SUSEJ
Red reading.

                              LEW
Oh. Anyway, the boss man's secretary, our representative
— – I have to laugh at that – – – do you think he
represents us? – – – dumb question, even for a blind man.
Anyway, she said he's in an important meeting.

                             SUSEJ
And you're not important?

                              LEW
My thoughts exactly! I say, "Who?" She says, "Lobbyists–
big important businessmen for the district". She then says–
"oil and textiles."

                            MAGGIE
We don't have oil here!

                            JACQUE
Or textiles! I ought to know.

                              LEW
Again, my thoughts exactly. Then they proceeded to shove
me, although politely, out the door. – Matt?

Matt stirs and sits up.

                             SUSEJ
Yeah.

                              LEW
Doughnuts?

SUSEJ

Yeah.

LEW

Someday he'll learn. – – – probably not.

MATT

Woo–hoo–ooh. What's going on? My head!

SUSEJ

Doughnuts.

MATT

Damn. Shit.

PETIE

(*Preaches*) Repent. Or repeat mistakes. Listen up. The red stuff – "Use not vain repetition, as heathens do; for they think that they shall be heard for much speaking." Hum? Same mistake over and over. Not Godly.

LEW

What's Petie on about?

SUSEJ

Being born again, again.

LEW

Oh, thought maybe Petie knew something.

IAIN

Lew – – – William Wallace. That's who? Yep, you remind me of him.

LEW

The Scot?

IAIN

Yeah.

JACQUE

Don't get him started.

LEW

How?

IAIN

He fought for the little man. A bonker of a lobbyist. Seems what Wallace fought against needs fought for again these days.

Screen 1007 – While Iain, Jacque, etc. talk show slides.
Alternate.

Big Screen	*Little Screen*
William Wallace statue	*Medieval battle charge*
– (Scotland)	
Knight's on horses	*Overcrowded with*
	– people scene (modern)
Crowded stock	*Crowded new suburban*
– exchange floor	*– housing project*

JACQUE

Pleeeease, Lew.

SUSEJ

Give Iain a break. He's only working on life's puzzle.

JACQUE

But he's missing too many pieces!

LEW

Well, I'm interested.

IAIN
(*Blurts out after a pause*) Who's our King? Anyone?

MAGGIE
Dog, it was. (*Speaking to Lew*)

LEW
Frog. – I could <u>see</u>.

MAGGIE
Dog!

IAIN
Got you! Don't I, huh? Don't know? You? You? (*Points at all the others very slowly*) You? Enough cuisine talk! Who's King?!

JACQUE
Expound Iain. You win.

1008 – As discuss Bravehart, show slides. Alternate.

<u>Big Screen</u>	<u>Little Screen</u>
King Edward I	*Queen*
Chinese Emperor	*Shaka*
– with Samurai warriors	
Templar Knights	*Boudeca*
Arab Warrior – Lawrence	*Skeleton straw man*
– of Arabia type or Saladin	*– icon (Scotland)*
CEO (fat suited rich guy)	

IAIN
No. Bear with me. It's like this. Like – Bravehart. You know.

MATT
Not really. Think I'll go back to sleep. (*Rolls up in his*

newspaper blanket)

IAIN

No! This is good! Listen! Maybe Susej can be our William Wallace.

SUSEJ

You want me to be Mel Gibson? I'm taller.

JACQUE

We don't have a King, remember, idiot?! We're a democracy. One man, one vote. Majority rules.

IAIN

Our King's top secret. Don't know our King. Wrong, wrong, wrong. It's wrong. Should know him. And, and, think of it like CEOs are today's Lords and the Sheriff of Notingham is the President. The king is over them all.

MAGGIE

Republic! We're a Republic! Majority rule? (*Shrugs her shoulders*) Well, maybe only an iffy Republic. Ballot stuffing. Computer tampering. Majority? Quasi Republic then.

MATT

Any more dandelions? (*Groans, then idly speaks*) Face it, politicians answer to someone. Think about it.

SUSEJ

Can't see me as a terrorist or kilted clod – so, let's not go there, subject change. Show of hands?

All raise hands.

MAGGIE

(*Says slowly*) True democracy here.

JACQUE

OK, OK. Change. But no politics! No merry men or nutty Scots. (*Said emphatically*)

IAIN

May have been nutty, but he was a 6 foot 7 inch nut. Yet, who is our King? But you're right, so I'll save if for another time.

LEW

Mel Gibson was 6 foot 7? (*Pauses*) Did you see the food line at St Mary's this morning? I did. (*Pause*) Weeelll, more heard, line went around the block.

MAGGIE

That's politics!

MATT

(*Talking from the blanket, not moving*) Ah, we could talk baseball.

MAGGIE

Love those Brooklyn Dodgers.

MATT

(*Still not moving – shouting quietly*) Hum, maybe not.

Man in trench coat, fedora, smoking unlit cigar slowly walks on stage. Looks at the group, says nothing, walks around nosing into stuff.

DETECTIVE I. B. LEEOWN

See anyone unusual today?

LEW

Nope. Seen no one. (*Holding up his cane*)

JACQUE
You're kidding, right? See that everyday. Weird people.

PETIE
Well, Detective I. B. Leeown, who's the prey tonight?

DETECTIVE I. B. LEEOWN
I ask the questions. Heard of any potential terrorist or
potential martyrs, scuttlebutt?

IAIN
Only from Matt there. (*Points to Matt laying down*) He
wished he'd of died awhile back.

DETECTIVE I. B. LEEOWN
Did he now. Why? Sympathizer? Potential battlefield
combatant? Terrorist?

IAIN
No. Doughnut overdose.

DETECTIVE I. B. LEEOWN
Don't get smart. (*Walks around silently then*) We need
citizen's help. Can't police everyone.

MAGGIE
Thank God.

DETECTIVE I. B. LEEOWN
What?

MAGGIE
Nothing. Just agreeing.

DETECTIVE I. B. LEEOWN
Good. All we know is they're atheist at best, heretics to
our ways, troublemakers out to do harm. Evildoers. Must

preempt their efforts. So, any help would be appreciated.

IAIN
Thought you just asked questions?

DETECTIVE I. B. LEEOWN
Christ, we're here to help you!

SUSEJ
We know.

MAGGIE
(*Laughing*) Ya, like check's in the mail.

IAIN
(*Chuckles*) Or love you as much in the morning as I do
tonight.

LEW
Be serious. Cops need our help. Anyone <u>see</u> more than
me?

ALL
No. No. No. No.

PETIE
Sorry officer, but we'll keep our eyes open.

DETECTIVE I. B. LEEOWN
These are dangerous people. Kinda see themselves as
gladiators for a cause. But reality is – they have no moral
values and are hypocrites.

JACQUE
We'll keep a sharp eye.

DETECTIVE I. B. LEEOWN
Remember, you're with us or against us. The world's the battlefield now. Think on it. (*On that, turns and slowly walks away*)

PETIE
(*Leaning to talk to Susej*) What do you think? Too close?

SUSEJ
We've time. Patience. Guess can't count on siren warning.

All is quiet after the detective leaves. Finally, Iain jumps up.

IAIN
(*Shouts*) Mirrors![1]

PETIE
(*Looks up from his book, stops page turning*) What the hell – – –?

IAIN
(*Pretends looking in mirror admiring self*) Ya.

JACQUE
Ya – what!

All stare at Iain with gestures of confusion. All start to talk but stops.

IAIN
(*After pause*) Buffalo mirrors. It's not politics or even Scottish.

---

[1] Mirror stories are adapted from Hyemeyohots Storm's <u>Lightining Bolt</u>, published by Ballantine Books,1994

LEW

I really do need to pass this way more often. I might see the light yet.

IAIN

You suggested a subject change. Remember? Wanted to talk about something else. Before the interruption.

SUSEJ

Iain, Iain, Iain.

IAIN

What?

MAGGIE

(*Stands up, assumes quick draw stance, hands poised to draw pistol*) Palabra Wild Bill or draw.

IAIN

Hell. What's going on?

All laugh uproariously.

SUSEJ

(*Stopping his laugh*) Mirrors, buffalo? Don't leave us hanging.

LEW

Let me guess. Buffalo need mirrors to perm their hair. Why it's kinky? Right? (*Laughing*)

IAIN

Don't be stupid.

All laugh again.

PETIE
Red – 'I am the way, the truth and the life. – – – I command you, that ye love one another – – –' (*Stops, ponders*) Could be: we is I and I is we?

LEW
You guys are nuts.

MAGGIE
Right! Get on with it, Iain.

IAIN
OK, OK. Long ago this Indian is following his young son who was turned into a buffalo – – –

All laugh.

LEW
Wheeze. Here we go again. (*Taps stick laughing*)

MATT
(*Lifts head*) Piotee story? Medicinal mushrooms, or something!

LEW
Got any, Iain? Helps seeing, I hear.

IAIN
No! Anyway, well, anyway the old man and his friends got tired tracking his son, and decide to sit on a knoll.

MATT
Piotee might help me, too. Whaddaya think, Lew?

IAIN
(*Acts out, ignoring Matt*) Well, the kid buffalo goes to the old men and says to get out – honcho buffalo is pissed and

will run them down, if they don't go.

MAGGIE

Is buffalo boy a buffalo or a boy now? Like elephant man?

IAIN

You're missing the point. Come on guys.

MATT

'allo, 'allo. (*Raises hand*) There's a point?

IAIN

Of course. Listen. So, the old man says he's too tired and
not afraid of Chief Curly Hairs. Stays put. His vision
quest prepared him, he says. But on seeing the bull – – –

MATT

This all sounds like bull – – – the kind associated with
flies.

LEW

Could I get my vision back on such a quest?

IAIN

(*Ignores Matt and Lew and continues*) Ooohhh. Seeing
the bull start to charge, one friend runs off, the other starts
to run, stops, starts, then decides to climb a tree and
observe. The old man sits and waits.

MAGGIE

So the bull tramples him and the bull and kid live happily
ever after in la la prairie land. The moral is – – –.

IAIN

(*Interrupts*) No, no! The bull stops just in front of the old
man, was testing his courage. Says, "You have a strong
heart, strong love." (*Iain stops speaking and moves closer*

to the fire to warm up)

MAGGIE
(*Watches Iain, aggressively looks around*) Well? What's the point? Ending? What happened next?

IAIN
Don't really remember.

MAGGIE
What?! Mental, that's what you are! Mental!

Screen 1009 – Start showing as Iain begins his old man being tested story. Alternate.

Big Screen	*Small Screen*
Herd of Buffalo	*White Buffalo*
Prairie Mouse	*Prairie Dogs*
Beaver	*Mirror – Multiple – reflections*

LEW
Know anything about those vision quests? Like to get some vision.

IAIN
It's not quite like that. Go 3–4 days, no food or water and God talks to you.

LEW
Done that, but not by choice, and no one said a damn word to me.

MAGGIE
Iaainn! The point?!

IAIN

Simple, actually.

MATT

Christ?!

SUSEJ

What?

MATT

Not simple to me.

MAGGIE

Go on, pleeeze!

IAIN

Well, (*Ponders some*) one man sees a fearless, courageous
person in the buffalo; the other a coward and the last sees
something inbetween. So, briefly, buffalo, Indians feel, are
mirrors we see ourselves in, whether good, bad or ugly.
What we do with this insight is up to us. The gift.
Nature's.

MAGGIE

(*Gets up, mimics looking in mirror*) Christ. Buffalo,
buffalo on the hoof who is the fairest of them all!

LEW

Blind man's gap! Worse than my generation gap. How do
I (!) know who I am in these looking glasses?

MAGGIE

Hopefully it's a metaphor or simile or litotes or parable or
parody or whatever.

IAIN

Replace buffalo with humans. How do we see <u>us</u> in other humans and how do we interact with <u>us</u>? We're all human mirrors. Of ourselves or something.

MAGGIE
Jesus, that's ridiculous.

SUSEJ
Not if think about it.

PETIE
Ya, sounds like this red print stuff here, love. Or I is we; we is I.

Walking on stage, with a light hearted flare in his step and general joy in attitude, is Nick.

NICK
How goes it with ya'll this fine evening? Ahh, is that delicacy I smell – canine, sautéed in left over French fry grease?

MAGGIE
Oh, shut up with your never ending mindless optimism.

LEW
Ahh, what mirrors do I miss here?

MATT
Broken ones.

NICK
What's this about mirrors?

MAGGIE
Don't ask. Buffaloes!

NICK

I see, I see!

LEW

Ya, ya. You would. (*Said huffily*) How about something in red for Nickie boy here?

PETIE

(*Holds book up and let's fall open – reads*) Verily, verily I say unto thee, when thou was young – (*Mumbles*) Thou walkest whether thou wouldest, but when old – (*Mumbles, mumbles then reads some more*) Another – carries whether thou wouldest not.

NICK

Damn. A prophet! Cause I sure as hell don't want to be here. But as happy men say – take what's laid out before you by the powers that be and make it work. (*Takes piece of food*) Hum, tastes like frog. Mmmm.

MAGGIE

Told you guys.

NICK

So, what's the topic tonight in this den of wayward followers?

IAIN

Nature. Oh, ya.

JACQUE

(*Slightly perturbed*) Iain! Yuu're beginning to frighten me. Youu tink nature haz all ze answers. Well, it doesn't.

IAIN

Why not?

JACQUE

It jus don't.

NICK

Christ, I love running into you guys. Good food, entertainment. Home away from home.

SUSEJ

Great.

IAIN

Way I see it, God created all this. (*Spreads arms and waves at all things*) Well, maybe not this exact spot. (*Kicks garbage nearby*) But nature, it stands to reason, encompasses His guides to life. Answers are given to us there. If we can read it.

Screen 1011 – While Iain talks of God's creation. Only on Big Screen and go through very quickly.

> *Big Screen*
> *Green forest up close – redwoods*
> *Raccoon*
> *Eagle*
> *Unique rocky edged mountains*
> *Beautiful plain*
> *Buffalo grazing*
> *Native American*
> *Crowd of People in city*
> *Rapid flowing river*
> *Pretty ocean scene*
> *Sky and sunrise*
> *Universe (stars)*

JACQUE

Look at all the garbage flies. Some nature. Humph!

MAGGIE

Speaking of flies, did anyone read the science section of last night's blanket? About fruit flies. (*Picks up rolled up paper they used for blanket*)

LEW

(*Tapping his white cane*) Let me think. Hmm. No, believe I missed it.

MAGGIE

Stop it, Lew. (*Chuckling*)

IAIN

(*Said with surprise, amazement*) Do you realize hermaphrodites are real? In human beings! Do exist?

NICK

What the hell? Where'd that thought beam in from?

IAIN

No. No. Bear with me. Bet there's more going on in nature than meets the eye! (*Said with excitement of new discovery*)

LEW

Ahh, wait a minute! Where're my glasses? I need to write this down. Iain – what's the word! Astonish.

IAIN

Well, I was just thinking – – –.

MATT

(*Speaks skyward and lays down*) Wonders never cease.

IAIN

– that if what we see is what we see –

MATT

Astonishing!!

IAIN

– and if actual physical(!) difference can naturally occur –

MATT

Like women and men?

IAIN

– why can't subterranean changes occur? It would be natural and a positive explainable force.

MATT

Sub – what?

IAIN

You know, hormones.

LEW

Ooh! You mean those women's feet you step on to make them moan? Ha, ha, ha.

MAGGIE

Leewww! Stop the dirty mind. Listen.

IAIN

Just thinking. If the physical part can develop like that, why can't internal parts? Subterranean. That's all.

JACQUE

Yuu mean gays are gays because that's nature's way. No! It's a choice! That's that!

LEW

(*Leaning toward Iain*) Hum, did Jacque just say

hermaphrodites don't exist?

JACQUE

Christ. No! Can't be! No!

SUSEJ

Never know. What's the paper say, Maggie?

MAGGIE

It's about gene manipulation in fruit flies.

JACQUE

Is diz about gay flies?

MAGGIE

Kinda.

JACQUE

Ooooh! Nooo!

MAGGIE

It's like this. They can put male genes in a female fruit fly body. During egg development or something, I guess.

JACQUE

Noooo!

MATT

(*Still laying down*) Talk about small. Hard, that must be.

MAGGIE

AND(!) vice versa. So, female looking male fruit flies were attracted to female looking female fruit flies. And vice–versa.

JACQUE

Christ? What's de world coming to?!

SUSEJ

About what it was.

MATT

<u>IT's</u> about time for Petie and his new-found book. Well, Petie?

PETIE

(*Drops book on ground, it flops open, reads open place*) It always seems to open to Matthew. Wonder if it's like a loaded dice book. Oh well.

NICK

Great!

PETIE

This is strange. I don't really get it. And it's in red, I guess He said it then. Listen, "for there are some eunuchs, which were so born from their mother's womb."

MAGGIE

How's that? Aren't eunuchs castrated males? Castrated in the womb???

MATT

(*Sitting up bewildered*) Sounds like it.

PETIE

There's more. Says – "and there be eunuchs, which have made themselves eunuchs for the kingdom of heaven's sake. He that is able to receive it."

NICK

Holy shit. In red!

MAGGIE

(*Walks around with dazed expression and mannerism*)

Who does it? (*Arms spread out*) Tiny, microscopic womb leprechauns? Midget gnomes of the womb. Sounds like a movie title.

PETIE

I don't know. Got me! I only read the red. Jesus's true words.

LEW

Yep. Love all! Easier for the blind. Things don't get in the way. Black, white, gay, petunias. All the same.

JACQUE

Nooo! (*Pulls at hair, looking up*) Can't be! Differences. Have to be!

MAGGIE

(*Laughing*) Face it Jacque, according to fruit fly genetics, we seem to have a new world order.

JACQUE

Not if I can help it. (*Pauses*) Damn liberals.

NICK

I see it now. Headline: Gnome Womb War declared. New threat to our homeland security. New Patriot Act required. Or an updated Protect America Act. We have a womb gap.

LEW

Hee, like I've said, huh Jacque, where's the inquisition when you need them? Popping out of nowhere and burning Maggie – like at the stake.

JACQUE

Eeeechhhg!!!

IAIN
Would these so called fruit flies be subterranean
hermaphrodites?

NICK
(*Chuckling*) You guys are strange. Inquisition bait. Like
Galileo, witches. Civilization's circle expands. Becomes
more inclusive. (*All movement stops and all stare at
Nick*)

*Screen 1012 – Start as Nick starts talking and continue during
pause. Alternate.*

Big Screen	*Little Screen*
Inquisition	*2nd Inquisition*
Gay couple	*Fruit fly*
Circle of Civilization drawing	

*Circle of Civilization – a large circle representing 'original
civilization' with words and symbols representing Greek and
Roman law and government inside circumference. Outside circle
are Christians, poor people, slaves, Galileo, witches, blacks,
women etc. Those who had difficulty getting freedoms and rights.*

MATT
(*After awhile staring at Nick*) Well, wasn't that special.
Any more food?

IAIN
Was that the cops? Hear anything?

SUSEJ
Not yet. Relax.

IAIN
Another mirror then? Night's still young.

MAGGIE

Mirrors. Mirrors. I'll never look at one the same again. Or
anything.

SUSEJ

Sure, Iain.

NICK

Remember last time I was here? Iain and Maggie were on
about Republican Kids. Or the lack thereof. I haven't
seen any either.

MAGGIE

(*Laughing smugly*) They don't walk around with tags on
their clothes. Tattooed foreheads. It was more a metaphor
about lousy, kid-unfriendly legislation, than actual kids.

LEW

Seems I've heard this somewhere, but then half–zheimer's
sets in occasionally these days.

MAGGIE

Pray you never reach the All–zheimer's stage.

NICK

Nah, stem cells will come to the rescue.

*Screen 1013 – Start to show slides while Lew says – "Seems – – –.
On big screen only.*

> <u>Big *Screen*</u>
> *Oocysts to stem cells chart*
> *Compare above with real photos of:*
> > *Frogs*
> > *Dog*
> > *Primate*
> > *Humans*

Show how all development is the same at this point.

Hear screeching tires, sirens, doors open, close. Detective I.B. Leeown rushes onto stage.

DECTECTIVE I.B. LEEOWN
Did you see them? Run by here?

PETIE
No. Just us.

DECTECTIVE I.B. LEEOWN
Reports say they dashed this way. Have them on the run and headed this way.

LEW
Nope. Saw no one.

DECTECTIVE I.B. LEEOWN
Have to be here.

JACQUE
If we saw these – what? – terrorists, we'd certainly speak up. Be good citizens. (*All give a chorus of yeses*)

MAGGIE
Check the creek down there. (*Points*) If ran that way, we wouldn't see anything.

DECTECTIVE I.B. LEEOWN
Could be. Check. (*Orders officer with him*) Damn evildoers. That's all they are. No principles. No point to what they do. They've cast the truth aside.

PETIE
Who's? Balzac's, Dickens', Browning's? Who's? Anyway, I read somewhere God's in all, so must be some good in

these radicals.

DECTECTIVE I.B. LEEOWN
Don't bet on it. Agents of Satan they are. No good.

MAGGIE
Harsh.

DECTECTIVE I.B. LEEOWN
No bleeding hearts crap. These are bad, soulless people.

MATT
'allo, 'allo, is that possible?

DECTECTIVE I.B. LEEOWN
Damn right it is. Burning at the stake is too good for these guys.

Voice off stage says "This way, chief." He takes off. Doors slam, cars speed away.

SUSEJ
The illusion continues. Another story, Iain? Wait. What's that book, Nick, sticking out of your pocket?

NICK
(*Looks surprised at pocket*) Oh, this. Forgot I had it. Found it in a garbage bin.

JACQUE
More educational budget cuts?

NICK
It's about Merlin. But, nothing like those crummy movies of our youth.

PETIE
Susej can I have a word in private?

They walk away from fire into another spot light.

PETIE
Do you think this group can do it?

SUSEJ
Sure, they're perfect.

PETIE
I don't know. Seem a little screwy to me. We need more
powerful people, big wigs. You know. Believable. Known.
Public eye people.

SUSEJ
Like us?

PETIE
We're different.

SUSEJ
Ya right. Petie, Petie, what am I going to do with you?

NICK
(*Talking about Merlin to the groups*) ——that's some of the
interesting parts of Merlin.

Susej and Petie arrive back in the group.

MATT
Weird Merlin story, yet, makes me think, the other day
when I stepped on an ant hill, did all the little ant people
scurry around screaming "why us"? (*In a high pitched
voice*) What ant offended God? God works in mysterious
ways! Why us? Force of nature! God's will. Pray for – – –

JACQUE

Go to hell Matt.

MATT

(*Gesture exaggerated*) Hump. And. Yes and.
Was I a force of Nature? – neat thought – or was I just
their God? Goddian Ant, so to speak. (*Said with dramatic
Roman forum style*) I am the Goddian Ant!

IAIN

Good grief.

SUSEJ

Seems you could be. Didn't we read somewhere God is in
all of us.

MAGGIE

You mean pejoratively or something. Spiritual.

SUSEJ

No, physical. Big Bang, primordial dirt is still with us, in
our genes.

MATT

What a thought. Big bang dirt genes.

LEW

Wow. Be something if the original trace minerals were
still there and passed on and on and on and on – – –

MAGGIE

Could happen.

SUSEJ

God. Truly, what a thought.

Suddenly, Leeown runs on stage and pulls Susej aside.

DETECTIVE I.B. LEEOWN
Susej, can we talk? Know you're up to no good. Trust me. Turn evidence.

SUSEJ
On what?

DETECTIVE I.B. LEEOWN
Terrorism. You guys want peace like I need more anal hairs. Give. We'll give you immunity. <u>Hell</u>, you might even be declared a national hero.

SUSEJ
Dreaming detective. Only want peace for all mankind. All!

DETECTIVE I.B. LEEOWN
Like Holy Shit you do. I've seen your kind before. On every profile list that exists.

SUSEJ
Terror and us is like rocking horse manure.

Offstage hear – "Inspector" – Leeown dashes off, yelling over his shoulder.

DETECTIVE I.B. LEEOWN
I'll get you.

NICK
That was heart warming. Oh well, Merlin, yes Merlin. He didn't know about lights or God's within, he only knew: <u>had to study Nature to know God</u>!

JACQUE
That's pagan! Damned evolutionist! Pagan!

NICK

Should we ignore the inspector that quickly?

SUSEJ

Of course. He's all wrong and knows it.

PETIE

Being wrong never stopped people like him before.

MAGGIE

Forever, practicing: obscene righteousness.

JACQUE

Evolution! (*Said liked dirty word*) I'm no damned
monkey. I'm no primate. I'm made after His image.
Remember!

LEW

Convenient for us, isn't it.

SUSEJ

Hummm? Jacque, you are a primate. Forget Leeown.

IAIN

Darwin, didn't he study carbuncles? Those little shell
things. Boat crust. Knew them babies inside out. His
theory was mostly a projection from that. I believe.

LEW

Face it, can <u>never</u> know the ultimate truth, the definitive.
<u>Never</u>.

SUSEJ

(*Exhales and shakes head*) God's way or Darwin's way.

LEW

Hold on, Darwin just studied God, so – same thing. Right?

Nature: God's true code. Bible.

JACQUE
Who cares?

MATT
'allo, 'allo – he studied that silent film star, Fatty
Carbunkle? Sex and evolution.

MAGGIE
Arbuckle! Arbuckle! Diabetes going to your ears?

MATT
Oh.

IAIN
Wait a minute. Just thinking, why would Darwin, Merlin,
scientists not want there to be a God? Like Nick said,
God's code's, nature, the true Bible. So, why not? (*All are
silent for awhile – nervous, anxious*)

JACQUE
(*Jumps in*) Science should discover wonders of God's
creation, not try and explain it away. So no God.

IAIN
Doubt it's their point.

JACQUE
A world without God – that's what scientists want. The
only world that exists to them.

MAGGIE
Hum? Doubt it. (*Pause – all quiet and blurts out*) The
Galileo problem! Yes! That's the issue! A bible reality
gap? Face it, no one knows how long the first four days
were. No sun, moon or stars till the fourth day! Like, no

day, as we know it. So, six days for creation takes on a new
meaning!

ALL

Huh? Huh? What? Hun?

IAIN

Hold on. Think we're only dealing with perspective here.
The <u>same</u> truth looks different, even though not,
depending on how you look at – perspective. Maybe we
do need this 'Nature God Code.'

Screen 1014 Start as Iain says hold on. Alternate. End with Matt
– yells in excitement.

<u>Big Screen</u>	<u>Small Screen</u>
Yellowstone Park	*Birds*
Ocean	*Insects*
Clean Beautiful Sky	*Fungus*
Rocky Mountains	*Redwoods*
Forest (Smokey Mt.)	*Bacteria*

MATT

(*Yells in excitement*) The poor gap! Not a Galileo gap.
Chuckie Dickens. Still see his visual pictures. Who has
the best poor? Yep!   Guess it's better than the missile gap
of cold war days.

Screen 1015 – Start after Matt says 'cold war days' and end with
Lew saying 'what about it Petie!'

<u>Big Screen</u>	<u>Little Screen</u>
Photos of people	*Dust storm*
– (of Dickens's time)	*Old poor*
More Dickens's time	*Dickens's school scene*
Street kids	*– sweat shops*
Modern inner city	*60's racist scene*

– (rundown school)
Depression scene kids

JACQUE

Without doubt, an undeclared war – that's this <u>poor gap</u>.
Trick is to keep the masses in the dark. In dark, with
Terrorism War and the like. Worked for the Romans.

MATT

Red Herrings – purple cows, blue horses. Definitely! These
wars.

LEW

What about it, Petie? Your book. Anything for us meek
and poor? Or is all as should be?

MAGGIE

The Ant God lurks!

LEW

Petie?

PETIE

(*Reading from the Bible, occasionally looking up*) Here.
Here. Try this on. The Big He preached about faults,
faults mind you, faults like having no needs, being rich.
Faults like having too many goods and says, "as many as I
love, I rebuke, and chasten: be zealous therefore, and
repent."

LEW

(*Said with high squeaky voice. Hand behind head*) Like
"Get behind me Satan." (*Calms*) Rich equals Satan. I like
it!

Detective I.B.Leeown walks out onto stage and moves arms as if
stopping run away horse.

DETECTIVE I.B.LEEOWN

Stay put. Don't move. It's down to the wire. Stay put.

NICK

Weren't going anywhere.

LEW

What's up?

DETECTIVE I.B. LEEOWN

Reliable evidence, says they're here. Right here! What
have you seen?

LEW

Nothing.

DETECTIVE I.B. LEEOWN

Can't protect you, if you don't help us. Think! Harder!
We need informers.

JACQUE

Nothing to think about. Harder or otherwise. Nothing's
going on here. No evildoers. Promise.

DETECTIVE I.B. LEEOWN

Simple terrorists, nothing more. They endanger our
existence. They cause division. They must be stopped.

NICK

Think you're looking in the wrong place. Nothing but
love here.

DETECTIVE I.B. LEEOWN

Love won't help here. Liberal pansy stuff.

LEW

Where's the light in all this?

DETECTIVE I.B. LEEOWN
Huh?

PETIE
You know. Children of THE LIGHT.

DETECTIVE I.B. LEEOWN
Look, just stay put. For your own good. We'll safeguard you. Remember, bitter fate awaits those who only serve self.

Detective I.B.Leeown leaves quickly from stage while giving darting looks in all directions.

NICK
What was that about?

LEW
I can't see.

MAGGIE
Nor me. What's he telling us?

PETIE
Probably that we're not what we think we are.

All are quiet – looking back and forth between each other.

NICK
Let's get back to Merlin. Was he a myth, <u>a figment</u>, or real?

Called from offstage.

S.P.
—— aaaaaaahh! He was no cookie! Fig Newton! Real. Real. Real. Absolutely. He was.

Enters grey bearded man, 15ᵗʰ century hat like wear today in college processions, tattered fake fur coat, walking stick about 6 feet high looking like the bug chasing burning lamps. Kind of acts like a pirate of the Caribbean in gestures and language.

SUSEJ

Thought you'd never get here. How's the business world?

S.P.

Dead. The Great illusion!

MAGGIE

(*Speaking out loud, but honestly searching*) God S.P., what are you, anyway? Eccentric – ya. Business failure – ya. Confused – most definitely. Demented – probably.

S.P.

Kiss my radishes. Try again. (*Always walking around, exaggerated, flamboyant, blurts out words*) Bull. Bull. Bull. Always the same. Generation after generation. No growth. Progress. No meat.

MAGGIE

See. Words. Like they mean something. Don't!

S.P.

(*Stops, looks at Maggie and in professional way says kindly*) Come on now, what is it? I have a lot of time, but little patience these days. (*All is quiet – long pause*) Welll? What do you want to know, Maggie?

MAGGIE

The truth! (*Shouts out, throws hands in air*) Ya! That's it!

S.P.

(*Hardily laughs – holds one hand up, other points to*

Maggie, nods head) Haaa! See? See? Yes. Christ! Don't demand much, do you? (*Laughs*)

MAGGIE

Ha! Fraud. Visions – Future – You – Pfui.

S.P.

See! This is what happens when ignore my vision!

Stage darkens to see screen better.

Must think. Definitely must think. Think. Think. Think.

Screen 1016. Show as S.P. says see what happens when ignore him. Ends as Iain says 'Balance? What? – – –

Big Screen	Little Screen
Knight around round table	Pollution (air)
WWII trench warfare	Trashed computer pile
Dead trees from toxic forest	Toxic dump
Dead battle field slain	Polluted oil rigs
Hiroshima after scene	Pagan symbol
Atomic bomb	2nd atomic bomb
Amazon jungle	

S.P.

(*Lights slowly come up, then slumps, becomes dejected – sits on crate, shakes head.*) Why does dodo, Triceratops, extinction fill my skull. (*Holds head*) Man, nature – far apart. So far, how will they ever understand?

IAIN

(*Finally shrugs shoulders, sheepishly says*) Balance? What? Need to balance the interaction? Man, nature? Are you saying? What?

S.P.

(*Balancing on one leg, flips to the other leg, arms wave*)
Aaaaghhh. Balance, you toad stool – it's needed.
Essential. Body – spirit. Balance. (*Turns in a circle,
moves arms like an airplane*) Instinct! Instinct. Yes.

*All aimlessly start walking, mumbling to selves. Hear a bunch of
disconnected words like instinct, balance, life, cigars, etc.*

S.P.

Reason! Pushaa. Nothing but instinct turned on itself.
Money, palaces, chariots. Reality? Only a deceptive
appearance of truth. Must look behind these tangible
things. For truth. (*Stops, puts hands on hip. Pirate pose –
waits for agreement or something*)

*Screen 1017 – Show while S.P. starts "Reason – – –" and as people
mill around. End after Jacque speaks.*

Big Screen	Little Screen
Pasture	N.Y. crowd
Lightening	Hummer
Forest	Rocket blast off
Sky (picturesque, heavenly)	Casino
Solitary person	Skelligs

JACQUE

(*Ignoring S.P.*) Maybe we should check out the job center.
Eat. What do ya think guys?

S.P.

(*Howls and exhibits physical antics*) OOOOOOOoaaach!
Damn Greeks. (*Shouts*) All their fault! Poisoned the
world.

LEW

How? What a hockey puck.

S.P.

Huh? Eeeeh! Making monetary things – Gods. That's
what they did. (*Said slowly in defeated tone*) Balance
shaken to the core.

MATT

You know, I believe, you're completely losing it, S.P.

S.P.

Haa, if you <u>think</u>, <u>believe</u> or <u>feel</u>, then you <u>know</u> –
nothing!

IAIN

Matt has a point. You really OK?

S.P.

(*Starts slow and pleasant, builds to anger*) But, it helps,
being a little strange. Seeing my way. (*Pauses –huffs and
puffs*) Especially – – – especially – when humans make the
sense of pixies flying underwater or, or, or spider web
umbrellas. Hoka Hee. Ya tee.

IAIN

Give us strength. Nature? Animals? What could a dumb
animal know anyway? <u>Where is man?</u>

S.P.

(*Starts doing tricks, conjuring, acts strange – simple things
like coin from ear, flowers out of a pocket, butterflies, any
kind of tricks with the crowd. Then picks up a rock and
reads from bottom of rock*) Made by God.

JACQUE

Knock it off. What's your point? If you have one.

PETIE

Wish I could help. But I believe we've outstripped the red

domain of this book. (*Keeps checking the book*)

S.P.

Irreconcilable differences – instinct and reason! See that, Petie, in your book yet?

PETIE

Hmmm. (*While looking at the book*)

MAGGIE

So?

NICK

Hold on. You saying, S.P., instinct a la Cro–Magnon Man or dog pissing on a fire hydrant trumps reason. And why we're where we are?

S.P.

(*Stops, hands on hips*) Give me a second on that imagery. As to your puzzle – I'd say, it's, well, more like poets! Yes, I'd say that's it – poets.

MAGGIE

And who understands them?

S.P.

See?

NICK

What? See?

S.P.

(*Starts spinning dances again, while spouts out singing soliloquy then stops like dancer finishing a routine and waits, hands out*) – Ta, daa. Nature speaks all the time. Animals are not subservient to man. Listen, open up to their messages. Tree messages, animal messages. Mineral

ones. Poets hear them. Yes they do. Instinct recognizes it
– mysterious signs. Balance! Regain that which was lost.
We need to rescue us from ourselves. Da, Da, Da, Daa.

Screen 1020 – Start slides as Nick says "See?" and continue as S.P.
sings soliloquy.

Big Screen	Little Screen
Dead buffalo	*Concentration camp oven*
Cut, dead trees	*Racism (clan hooded mob)*
Mining pollutions	*Glaciers gone*
Ocean pollution	*River pollution*
Overcrowded homes	
– development abutting forest or estuary.	

NICK
Da, da my ass. You're nuts. Besides, you're going too fast.

S.P.
(*Moves, talks in slow motion*) Hooow maaannnyyy ooofff
– (*Etc., keeps it going at this slow rate*) – you are there? 5
to 7 billion. Oooh. Evolution's – too late. Oooh.

JACQUE
This is worse than watching grass grow.

S.P.
(*Still in slow motion mode*) Looook, aaaa,
uuuunniivversaal aaabbbyyysss –looook. (*Points at screen*
and sees present city and morphs into Mad Max-like city)

Screen 1020B – As S.P. points, have modern city like N.Y.C. and
flash back and forth with Mad Max city, as morphing.

S.P.
(*Pulls Susej aside*) Seems I was not much help.

SUSEJ

Who knows? This world's struggling. Torn apart by hate, fanaticism, racism, violence, greed, contempt for harmonious equilibrium. Did they ever read It? We need a new way. They must realize: no balance, no life possible on earth. This species <u>does</u> need to rescue itself.

S.J.

Come on, it's been worse. (*Turns to the gang*) I bid you adieu. (*Said to all and salutes*) State of bliss to you all. (*Yells*)

As S.P. leaves, hear sirens again and getting louder.

PETIE

Now?

SUSEJ

Yes, now.

PETIE

For sure.

All get up and leave.

SUSEJ

(*Said as walking away*) Yes.

LEW

(*Being helped by Maggie*) Yes, yes. Who said it, Keats, no Faulkner – My mother the fish.

CURTAIN FALLS

THE END OF ACT ONE.

ACT II

SETTING: 1000 years into the future. On a Martian outpost. Reddish Martian color prevades all set. Painting in back is of Mars, illusion of geodesic dome where people are housed. Only one screen on upper stage left. Irrelevant standing on a bolder with notebook. Nick with large book, scrolls to side, writing down what is said. Everyone holds copies of printout. Wear togas.

Throughout Act II have people talking fast, over each other at times, interrupting etc. Keep moving fast.

MAGGIE
(*Shouts*) Irrelevant!

IRRELEVANT (SUSEJ)
Wait. Wait. Give me a chance. Let me finish. "On the rock I will" – – – no, no. Need something new, catchier for the age.

MAGGIE
Master Irrelevant! This start needs changed too. "Behold the end is – – –." Was misleading anyway.

IRRELEVANT (SUSEJ)
Not very poetic to say "Behold, you're going to die. Some soon, some later, some much later. So, to do right, use death as an advisor. The end is near."

LEW
(*Sings Christmas tune*) – – – And be good for goodness sake. Oh, you better watch out, you – – –

IRRELEVANT (SUSEJ)
Come on, come on, gotta get serious.

IAIN

Damn! (*Looks at his rewrites, hold up. Interrupts*)
This death thing. "Thou shalt not kill." What didn't they
get? Thought it was simple enough.

NICK

Maybe we should just do a DVD. Pictographs or
something. Real simple stuff, visual. Implant nanobots!

IAIN

How about adding after – "thou shalt not kill" – a comma
and then <u>no</u> ifs, ands, buts or exceptions. And <u>no</u> murder.

PETIE

Will it still be <u>my</u> rock?

IRRELEVANT (SUSEJ)

No. You need a rest. Maggie's turn.

PETIE

Great! I like the idea! As to DVDs, out. Everyone
doesn't have electricity, yet. Face it, not much has
changed for our camel eyed people.

LEW

Cro–Magnon's fault, this lack of camel eye understanding.
Why'd that strain evolve?

MATT

Vicious little tikes, weren't they? So, violent.

LEW

– Oh why – why couldn't man see, controlling his inner
Cro–Magnon was crucial?

IRRELEVANT (SUSEJ)

Focus people. Let's go. Focus. The New Testament was to

simplify, clarify the Old Testament Laws, but fell short. And why this new effort. The New, New Testament. It's overdue. <u>So focus</u>! (*Said with anger*)

JACQUE
How about nature again?

PETIE
Na. Not much nature left, anyway. Would almost need to <u>completely</u> start again. Don't want that – yet. <u>Do we</u>?

MATT
Ya, books still seem best. Nature's a brain twister for them.

MAGGIE
This rewriting is hard. Simple, plain already – love thy enemies – simple.

LEW
It's that Cro–Magnon. I'm telling you.

MAGGIE
(*Stops writing, slumps*) Ya. What are there 12 – 15 –20 billion people now? Why not a <u>Love Army</u>? (*Acts dramatic*) Truly, be all you can be? One billion. Peace Army of Love. PAL. See it now. PALS descend in mass. One billion pounce on conflicts peacefully.

NICK
I see it too. Have to run out of bullets trying to kill them all. Ya, peace, then's inevitable.

MAGGIE
One billion would scare the shit out of any dictator. Ultimate sit–ins. Gandhi's reborn!

NICK

Man desperately needs to think outside the box. Any box. Shit, ya.

LEW

Got that one right. Don't want to hear – billions needed to defend self. This is a species problem! Don't they see?

JACQUE

Time's short. Our escape pod will soon be found.

IRRELEVANT (SUSEJ)

Where are we?

PETIE

Maybe I'm dumb or something, but what was the point of that red stuff anyway? You know, the red words.

S.P.

Love. All are one. Something like that. That's all.

MATT

(*Singing*) I hear noises, but no one's there.

IRRELEVANT (SUSEJ)

Good. Still time.

PETIE

Maybe we did complicate it too much. With church stuff. Words. Know what I mean?

MAGGIE

Well, let's review. Weed out superfluous. Pare down.

IAIN

Irrelevant.

IRRELEVANT (SUSEJ)
Yes.

IAIN
No. Look, light's irrelevant. Like Thomas' Gospel, one of those torched Gospels, said, "Kingdom of heaven is like a mustard seed. The smallest of all seeds, but when falls on prepared soil, it grows into a large plant."

MAGGIE
If didn't get love in all things or light in all, their neuron couldn't possible see this one. Them, God, in a mustard seed. Together, grow as one, are one. Forget it.

MATT
'allo, 'allo ——you're saying God is a mustard seed?

JACQUE
Get out. Plant ovum?

MATT
Works for me. Let's get out of this manmade orchard. Let's go.

IAIN
People are mustard seeds? Weird.

JACQUE
Aaaahhhhh! This is nowhere. Irrelevant?

IRRELEVANT (SUSEJ)
Patience. People are unaware of their inner God.

PETIE
Check out Thomas again. Why they chucked this Gospel, I don't know. Listen, in red, if had red. Thomas: Thee, "living Jesus himself changes those who mistake the

kingdom of God for another worldly place." (*Acts like reading and skipping places*) Blah, blah, blah, blah – – – if look for the Kingdom in the sky, the birds will get there first – — blah, blah, blah – – – if in the sea, fish will be there before you.

IAIN
This is silly. Thomas seems nuts. Chuckable. Definitively. They were right.

PETIE
(*Ignores Iain and continues more excited as goes*) Blah, blah, blah, – – – What you look forward to has already come, but don't recognize. Blah, blah, blah – —. It is here. Blah, blah – – –. Son of Man is within.

S.P.
The Mustard Seed! I get it!

NICK
You're kidding? Right?

S.P.
(*Really excited*) Get it? "The Living Jesus," gift, is in all of us. Like mustard plant stuff is in mustard seeds. And mustard seed stuff is in the plant.

NICK
Get real, S.P.

MAGGIE
Isn't that just genes?

S.P.
Bingo! Primordial gook.

JACQUE

Is this a tangent? Helpful?

LEW

Speaking about tangents, does anyone know what the
name Thomas means?

IAIN

Who cares? Well, Tom might I guess.

LEW

Twin.

IAIN

Big deal. They have to be here soon and we seem
nowhere. Can we get serious?

LEW

But we are. If Thomas had red print, it would say Jesus said
something like, "you are my twin, examine yourself and
learn who you are – – –." How about that now?

MATT

'allo, etc. We should all be doubters then – doubt it.

S.P.

No, no. That was propaganda. Like yesterday's political
attack ads.

JACQUE

Thomas was too radical. Divine light was all we were, he
implied.

PETIE

(*Reading pile of papers*) Says here, he said, "All have
direct access to God through divine images within us."
Imagine being the light, Iain? People?

NICK

Whoo! Priest's problem again.

PETIE

Listen, John, on other hand, professes –

MAGGIE

(*Cuts in*) Hold it, according to John's words, the light is
never really seized. Man dark, God light? And never the
twain shall meet. I don't know how it helps.

S.P.

Does make a church important.

LEW

Church is not Godly or whatever.

MATT

(*Grunts as sits up*) Huh? Is that a koan or something?
Oxymoron?

JACQUE

Let's be serious.

IAIN

Koan? Could be. Believe in Jesus to find divine truth – so
sayeth John.

MAGGIE

Limiting, isn't it?

Sirens in background.

LEW

I may be blind, but does anyone else hear that noise? The
pod's found.

MATT

'allo, 'allo – not much time – – – whadda we do?

Petie holds hand up.

IRRELEVANT (SUSEJ)

Yes, Petie?

PETIE

Well, don't think the "I am" worked. I am the way – I am
the truth – I am the light – I am the vine – I am the water
of life – – –. Need more than <u>mutual support</u>, so to speak,
to face hatred and persecution.

S.P.

Got that right.

NICK

Dividing is never good.

MAGGIE

Petie, pull out that Phillip Gospel.

LEW

You mean Mary's?

MAGGIE

Whatever. But didn't whoever say, "Jesus said discover the
light within – you are from the kingdom."

S.P.

Awesome thought – implies you <u>are</u> your neighbor, light,
God. Hard to kill yourself then.

IAIN

Kill neighbor, thus self. Sounds like suicide. Could be
onto something.

MAGGIE

But isn't that what they're doing?

S.P.

Irrelevant! We've got to think of something that can connect! (*Pause*) Or all is lost.

IRRELEVANT (SUSEJ)

Yes. I hear. Think. Think. What connects all whether Hindu, Muslim, Buddhist, atheist, Mormon, Catholic, Christian, bumbula or whatever? Inclusive!

NICK

Seized or not seized, that is the question.

S.P.

What the hell?

NICK

Ya, the light. Did the divine light get into us or not? That is the question. Thomas vs. John. Seized or not seized. That is the question.

JACQUE

This is getting us nowhere. Now we're going to define light – love.

S.P.

Is that necessary? Definitions!

MAGGIE

(*Nervous – walks around*) Maybe. Maybe. But what do we do? Time's running out.

NICK

Are we even asking the right questions?

Sirens in background.

S.P.
Why? Why? Every time we try to regroup in some vineyard setting the cops pressure us.

LEW
Ya, I can smell them.

MAGGIE
Maybe that's why we never get it quite right. We're always rushed.

NICK
What about that Gospel of Truth?

PETIE
(*Shuffles through papers, pulls out scroll*) You mean Gospel of Truth is Joy. Use the whole title, please.

NICK
Ok, Ok! But does it help?

S.P.
Gospels, gospels, gospels, they're all close, but shit really. No cigars.

JACQUE
Blasphemy.

MATT
Where's that damn Inquisition when need them. 'allo, 'allo. (*Yells*) Yo! Inquisition! Inquisition!

MAGGIE
Oh, shut up. They're close enough.

JACQUE

Missing something – damn. What?

MAGGIE

A point, maybe.

IRRELEVANT (SUSEJ)

(*Jumps on rock, arms outstretched, preaches*) Let one who
seeks not stop until he finds. When he finds, he will be
troubled. When troubled he will be astonished and will
rule overall.

MAGGIE

That's old Tom's stuff. Why go there?

PETIE

Mary had real vision. A real woman who knew all, I quote
– "The Son of Man is within you. Follow after him!"

S.P.

No, no, no. Verbiage. What's it all mean? Words, no
heart. No connection to its audience.

MAGGIE

Good as any old junk. Simple.

LEW

(*Waves cane in air*) Right on! Humans can't handle the
complicated or the subtle. Or innuendos. Parables,
metaphors. They need facts. Just the facts. Wordless
words. Simple.

IAIN

Ya like, like – well like you know you know, but you don't
know what you know, yet you know you know.

S.P.

Got something there Iain. Like an orgasm. (*Looks around, all look blank and challenges*) Explain one! Go ahead. Tell me. Can't, huh? Words fail. You know, but don't know what ya know. That's an orgasm.

JACQUE

This is hopeless.

LEW

No, no.

JACQUE

Yes! Yes! The powerful Cro–Magnon will always manipulate words to their ends. Point is lost on them.

IRRELEVANT (SUSEJ)

(*Speaks from rock again. Keeps jumping up, down, walks around thinking*) Here it is – – – in the beginning was the word. Well, not exactly, really it was a big burst of light and became all things – – –.

MAGGIE

OK, now we're getting somewhere. Geesh.

IRRELEVANT (SUSEJ)

To continue – Therefore it's not a good idea to piss Him off. You know He's getting tired and could withdraw this light and – – –.

MAGGIE

Hold on, hold on. Maybe that's the wrong tack. Threats are not helpful.

NICK

(*Hold arms out to side and turns*) Right Maggie. But it's paramount to realize it's here. All here. Pick a rock up and look underneath and doesn't say "made by God," but "Hello, I'm God, too." Like the movie? That's all need.

IAIN

Even a simple-minded species should get that.

MAGGIE

Brilliant! Need to say – fools, listen up. It's here, here, here. Stop the suicides. That's the Book we need. Basics for the <u>New, New Testament</u>.

JACQUE

That's the love part.

MAGGIE

But it didn't work! Love's too abstract.

NICK

What <u>is love</u> anyway? Light?

MATT

Irrelevant.

IRREVELANT (SUSEJ)

Yes! Irrelevant. It's really that self and enemy <u>are</u> the same being, not love that should be the focus.

MAGGIE

That sounds stupid.

S.P.

Could be, could be. Maybe Irrelevant's on to something. Consider reverence for all life; or anything that promotes life. Accept life is mysterious and precious. All life. Promote it. Have reverence. Be engrossed in the 'being alive' episode.

PETIE
Should I be writing this part down?

IRRELEVANT (SUSEJ)
Probably.

MAGGIE
Remember we want this gospel short. Simple! The fools.

S.P.
Makes sense to me. Answers their burning question about abortion, anyway. Sometimes it promotes life and good. Sometimes it doesn't – and bad. Simple.

IAIN
Huh?

Screen 1022 – Start showing as Nick talks and show Gospels of Gnostics scripts, NAG find, Dead Sea Scrolls.

> *Big Screen*
> *4 or 5 examples*

NICK
Why did they get rid of so many Gospels, anyway?

LEW
As I see it, some guy, Irenaeus Bishop of Lyon, decided around 170 CE to have four! Four he selected. Later others reinforced his selection. By a vote of 24 to 15, with 17 abstentions.

IAIN
Control! That's what it's about. Too much individual freedom otherwise.

MATT
No. Too open for interpretation. Lost church control.

That's why other Gospels had to go.

                    S.P.
Phillip says – It's simple, an initiation – just go down to the
river and say I am a Christian – voila – Baptized –
initiated.

                  MAGGIE
Come on now! Must be more than that.

                    MATT
See what I mean?

                    S.P.
Phillip says, like a new born is meant to grow in faith
toward love, hope, understanding.

                    LEW
Sounds like a better deal than confession.

                    S.P.
No. No. Phillip says faith is our earth to root in. Hope is
water for nourishment, love is air to grow in.

                  MAGGIE
And that's not confusion, stupid. I see why the inquisition
flourished.

                    S.P.
Then says – after baptized one becomes a transformed
believer and no longer Christian. But Christ!

                  MAGGIE
Get the wagons. Here comes Irenaeus. Inquisition time.
Look, this tack would probably produce an elite; a
pompous, arrogant, bastard elite to boot.

LEW

Really, truly doesn't seem inclusive, does it?

NICK

Maybe we should move on to Mary's Gospel.

MAGGIE

Why? One's as vague as the other. Life promoting? Love? Ha!

S.P.

Mary's focus was – let no one lead you astray – – –.

MATT

Brilliant so far.

PETIE

Should I begin writing again?

EVERYONE

No!

MATT

Any specifics on being lead astray?

S.P.

Jesus said, she says, said, "Lo here or Lo there –
– –" (*Chuckles*)

MATT

Ahh! Clearer.

JACQUE

Maggie's right. We need a functioning document for
humans. Simple. Specific. Clear cut. Can't leave it to
their imagination or interpretation.

PETIE

You'll let me know when to write, won't you.

EVERYONE

Ya, ya, ya, ya.

S.P.

Mary then spends a lot of time on visions.

IRRELEVANT (SUSEJ)

Let's not go there this time. Fraud comes to mind and taunts like – (*Said in whining, singing voice*) "My vision's better than your vision's." Ha – ha –ha. God! Humans!??

S.P.

Says here in Gospel of Truth.

Others try to stop him from speaking.

S.P.

No, no – this might help us, says – it's a little long –

MATT

Try us – what else do we have?

S.P.

Well, Truth, says basically, "God should not be viewed as petty."

IAIN

I don't get it.

S.P.

Well, Truth says basically, "God should not be viewed as petty, nor harsh, nor wrathful like portrayed in some biblical stories, but as a being without evil." Further says,

"Picture Holy Spirit as God's breath and imagine this breath breathing forth an entire universe of living beings and then drawing all beings back to an embrace of their divine source."

MAGGIE

Geesh. That was a bit much.

NICK

Why didn't that Lyon's Bishop like this stuff, Gospel?

S.P.

Truth ends suggesting, "discover God in themselves and themselves in God.

IAIN

These trashed, excommunicated Gospels do seem to have a 'singular' focus, as Holmes would say.

MATT

Say what?

IAIN

Holmes always said 'singular' this, 'singular' that. (*Laughs*) I like it. Wanted to use it. For focus.

MATT

Iain, Iain, Iain, no wonder we fail.

JACQUE

Is this getting us anywhere?

PETIE

Short. This is going to be the shortest Bible ever. My pen forgets its function.

NICK

Maybe we can usefully use paintings, pictures, as filler, to
bulk up this New, New Testament.

IAIN

Heavy. Weight. Means intellectual book. Ya, people like
that, will take it more serious. Need a heavy book.

NICK

That wasn't my point, Iain. The cops are closing in and we
have nothing. The end nears. Pictures might be our
answer.

PETIE

That's a point.

S.P.

OK, Ok. What about Jesus' secret writings, should we go
into them?

EVERYONE

No.

S.P.

How about the Gospels of Paul, the Savior, Joel, Andrew,
James or whoever, should we check those out?

EVERYONE

No!

S.P.

Should we get into that Round Dance of the Cross or just
avoid it?

MATT

'allo, 'allo. Remember the Lyon Bishop and his notty,
notty notties, remandings.

NICK

Ya, humans can't handle it. Fun and humor aren't that species' strong point.

JACQUE

But, that feet washing thing was important, if confusing. It was a sharing, brought us together before He left.

MAGGIE

(*Showing excitement*) Ya, but it left out the best part. Dancing! Singing!

LEW

(*Shows wonderment, spreads hands out*) Can see it now. After we ate, held hands in a big circle and sang and danced the night away. Zorba would have been jealous.

MAGGIE

What a night. A cosmic dance. The original Irish wake.

IAIN

I never understood.

MAGGIE

(*Dancing, speaks in a praising voice*) We know. Your loss, but we celebrated life. We become part of the whole. We recognized the mystery, get it – mystery. One!

PETIE

My pen's in limbo here, folks.

NICK

Maybe we should get back to mirror analogies again.

IAIN

Hell no! That's even worse. Buffaloes? Too intellectual.

MAGGIE

Remember that line He sang in the Round Dance?
(*Singing, jingly*) "I am a mirror to you, who know me.
Aaaa Meeen."

MATT

Yep. And all lost. Blame Irenaeus.

PETIE

(*Yells*) What do I write!? Come on! So far I have one
sentence. Get it? The New, New Testament awaits.

JACQUE

Yaaa. (*Sounds like groan*) But, we need more!
Something!

PETIE

Enough, enough. Testament by committee sucks. Thomas
is my man. I'll decide. Dictate. Here goes. First he said
<u>He</u> – (*Points skyward*) said, "If don't know yourself, then
you live in poverty, you are poverty."

LEW

Too open to interpretation. Again!

PETIE

(*Angrily*) Just listen! Then he said, <u>He</u> said, "Recognize
what is before your eyes, and the mysteries will be revealed
to you." How about that, huh?

IAIN

Sounds like that mirror stuff or nature.

PETIE

Shuush. Maybe, just thinking out loud here, we could
make Thomas' <u>whole</u> Gospel the New, New Testament.
Only 114 verses.

MAGGIE

Then we're back where started, just different, not necessarily better.

NICK

(*Shuffling through papers*) Has a point. Some of this Thomas makes no sense anyway, like – "whoever does not hate father and mother cannot be my disciple – ."
(*Shrugs*) Do the negatives cancel out here, <u>or what</u>?

IAIN

Here's a mirror quote, unreal – says, "When you see your likeness in a mirror you are pleased."

MAGGIE

So? This stuff's vague as fog. Just like the old New Testament.

PETIE

I'll only take the <u>clear cut</u> stuff then.

NICK

Then you'd be just like that Lyon guy.

PETIE

(*Walks around reading Thomas, acts like lecturer*) Let me read this anyway – more Thomas. First he says, "Who has found the world and has become wealthy, let him renounce the world. – – – Why do you wash the outside of the cup? – – – Do you not understand the one who made the inside also made the outside – – –."

JACQUE

Petie, where are you going with this?

PETIE

(*Stops, looks around, but ignores Jacque and continues to*

read, preach from papers) – – – You shall enter the
Kingdom when you make two into one, – – – when you
make inner like outer and outer like inner and the upper
like lower and when you make male and female into a
single one, so that male will not be male nor that female be
female, then you will enter the Kingdom.

MAGGIE
Interpretations. And wild ones! That's what that would
produce. (*Laughing*) Ha, ha, ha! I'm speechless.

NICK
Devious people could make just about <u>anything</u> they
wanted out of that verbiage. Like churches who declared
<u>their</u> "religion's" traditions: <u>The only truth</u>. Cro–Magnon
lurks in all.

LEW
Yep, lot of wars in that view. Just take England alone.
Mary then Elisabeth. All the needless burnings.

LEW
Such cruel, <u>cruel</u> wars justified against those who wouldn't
salute their tradition. Shame, shame, shame.

NICK
Need to avoid that again, for sure. Thomas won't do it.

MAGGIE
Ok, ok. Focus. What are we trying to accomplish with
this document anyway? Huh? What?

MATT
Right, we need a focus.

JACQUE
Little late for that, isn't it. We need a gospel. The truth.

Not a focus.

IAIN
Based on what?

MATT
'allo, 'allo. What's that movie line? You know. Ya.
Human's can't handle the truth!

MAGGIE
What are we getting at?

JACQUE
Wait– wait!

MAGGIE
But our question remains, what are we trying to show.
Isn't it – Who is He – (*Points up*) For us today?

NICK
Could be.

PETIE
How the dickens do I scribe this?

MATT
Words will fail, won't they?

JACQUE
Questions – Can words provide the power of "His" –
(*Points up*) – experience? Can we participate in that
experience? Can – – – .

MAGGIE
Sorry, but that's it! Look!

EVERYONE

Huh?

JACQUE

(*Yells*) They're coming! (*Points*) And close! Times up!

All scurry around collecting stuff to leave.

JACQUE

What do you have Petie, for this <u>New, New Testament</u>?

PETIE

(*While all still scurry, stands and reads loudly*) Here it is,
the New, New Testament: In the beginning, (*Pauses*) –
there was a burst of divine light or divine breath or divine
geologic gook and <u>become all</u> things. That means <u>it's</u> you,
your neighbor, your stranger, earth, trees, the whole
shebang. All things! Humankind's denominator is one.
No differences. So, unless you're pathologic or psychotic,
<u>act accordingly.</u> Absorb life; and being alive. Breathe it
in.

IAIN

That's it? <u>It</u>! That's not even elegant.

PETIE

Yep! But that's the <u>New, New Testament</u>.

NICK

You could put that on a small business card.

PETIE

(*Shrugs shoulders*) Don't need more. Really. Great, huh?

MAGGIE

Guess so, the other stuff <u>is</u> like country borders – – – <u>all</u>
<u>made up</u>.

JACQUE
Can't do any more. We're finished.

IRRELEVANT (SUSEJ)
Let's go! (*All slowly start walking away*) Here they come.

All run.

IRRELEVANT (SUSEJ)
Petie let's go, <u>run</u>.

PETIE
I need copies. A batch, I'll catch up. Must mail.

All exit stage except Petie.

IRRELEVANT (SUSEJ)
(*Yell from off stage*) Petie, we'll do it later.

Cops run on stage, grab and cuff Petie.

DETECTIVE I.B. LEEOWN
Here's one, anyway. Cuff him. Damn heretics. Terrorists.
At least, one neck will stretch. Burn that stuff. Papers.

*Stage mists up with heavy cloudy mist, thunder, all disappear as a
bright orange–red light invades stage and audience. Then on
main screen behind rock an atomic bomb blasts (multiple shots)
are shown. Then all is dark. Then on big screen show (in slow
succession) slides of space, stars, planets → ocean → trilobite →
dinosaurs → dodo → fish → crustaceans on land → frog → mice
→ deer → bear → primate → Neanderthal → Australopithecus
→ modern man → crowd of men. Bomb again (shortly after
crowd seen) Same orange–red light. Then black again. Then go
through all photos again but faster. Then black again. Wait 10
seconds in dark then words on big screen. "NEXT TIME?" → just
show bomb blast this time → goes black and after appropriate time*

(5 seconds) project "THE END."

CURTAIN FALLS

THE END